READING CHAMPION

Kind Kitty

by Katie Dale and Daniele Fabbri

W
FRANKLIN WATTS
LONDON • SYDNEY

Long ago, there lived a kind woman called Kitty. She loved to make people happy.

She had one son, Tom, who was a sailor.

He spent many months at sea.

Soon Tom would be coming home.

So Kitty decided to make him

his favourite treat – apple pie.

She went to the cupboard ...

3

... but all her apples had gone rotten!

Kitty frowned.

"Hmm ... I do have a lot of nice carrots," she said thoughtfully. "Maybe I could sell some at the market. Then I could buy some fresh apples for Tom's pie."

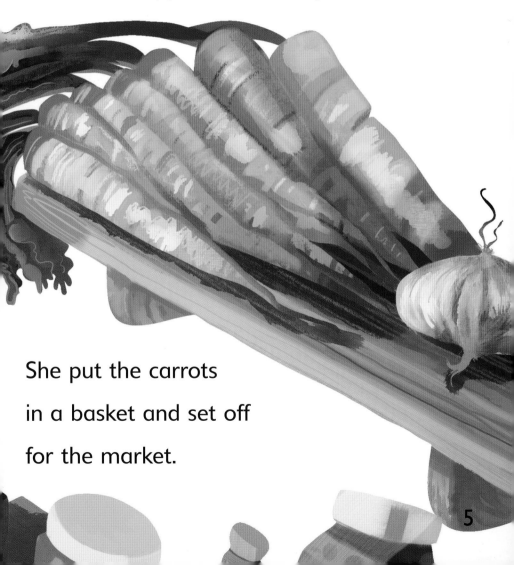

She put the carrots
in a basket and set off
for the market.

Outside, the birds were singing.

Kitty smiled as she walked down the road.

But then she saw a man looking very sad.

Kitty frowned.

"Whatever is the matter?" she asked.

"I wanted to make my wife a cherry cake

for her birthday," the man said. "But

the birds have eaten all my cherries!"

"Oh no!" Kitty said. She didn't like

seeing anyone looking so sad.

"I can help you," Kitty said. "Would you like my carrots? You could make a carrot cake instead."

"Oh, thank you!" the man cried. "My wife loves carrot cake."

Kitty smiled. Making others happy always made her happy too.

"I must give you something in return,"
the man said, looking around. "Would
you like some flowers?"

"Thank you," Kitty replied.

Maybe she could sell the flowers
at the market. Then she could buy
some apples for Tom's pie.

Kitty smiled as she walked over the hill to the market. It was a lovely sunny day.

But after a while, Kitty saw a woman looking sad.

"My dear, whatever is the matter?" Kitty asked.

"I bought these chocolates for my sick grandmother," the woman sighed. "But they have melted in the sun. Now I have nothing to give her."

"Oh no!" Kitty said. She hated to see anyone looking so sad.

"I can help you!" Kitty said. "Take
your grandmother these flowers instead."
Kitty gave the woman her flowers.
"Oh, thank you!" the woman cried.
"She will love them!"
Kitty smiled. Making others happy always
made her happy too.

"I must give you something in return."

The woman took an apple out of her bag

and gave it to Kitty.

"Thank you," Kitty replied.

Now she could make a small apple pie as

a treat for Tom!

As Kitty walked home, she passed
a donkey looking sad.

"Poor donkey. Are you hungry?"
Kitty asked.

She looked at her apple. It would make
a small treat for Tom. But it would be
a good meal for the donkey.

"I can help you," Kitty said.

She gave the donkey the apple.

"Hee-haw!" the donkey brayed happily.

Kitty smiled. Making others happy always

made her happy too.

But now she had no treat for Tom.

Sadly, Kitty headed home.

15

When Kitty got back home, Tom was already there.

"Tom!" Kitty cried. "How wonderful to see you!"

She hugged him tight.

"I wanted to bake your favourite treat," Kitty said. "But I didn't have any apples. I'm so sorry."

"Don't worry, Mother," Tom said, smiling. "I'm just happy to see you."

Kitty smiled too.

"But I do have a gift for you," Tom said, giving Kitty a box.

Kitty opened the box and looked inside.

"An apple pie!" she laughed.

"How wonderful!"

Tom smiled. Making others happy always made him happy too.

Story order

Look at these 5 pictures and captions.
Put the pictures in the right order
to retell the story.

1

Kitty helps the donkey.

2

The apples are all rotten.

3

The chocolates are melted.

4

Tom has a pie for Kitty.

5

Kitty sees the sad man.

Independent Reading

This series is designed to provide an opportunity for your child to read on their own. These notes are written for you to help your child choose a book and to read it independently.

In school, your child's teacher will often be using reading books which have been banded to support the process of learning to read. Use the book band colour your child is reading in school to help you make a good choice. *Kind Kitty* is a good choice for children reading at Purple Band in their classroom to read independently.

The aim of independent reading is to read this book with ease, so that your child enjoys the story and relates it to their own experiences.

About the book

A very kind woman called Kitty heads to the market to trade her carrots for some apples to make her son an apple pie. Along the way, she spreads cheer and generosity.

Before reading

Help your child to learn how to make good choices by asking:
"Why did you choose this book? Why do you think you will enjoy it?"
Look at the cover together and ask: "What do you think the story will be about?" Ask your child to think of what they already know about the story context. Then ask your child to read the title aloud. Ask: "What are some kind things you've done this week?"
Remind your child that they can sound out the letters to make a word if they get stuck.
Decide together whether your child will read the story independently or read it aloud to you.

During reading

Remind your child of what they know and what they can do independently. If reading aloud, support your child if they hesitate or ask for help by telling the word. If reading to themselves, remind your child that they can come and ask for your help if stuck.

After reading

Support comprehension by asking your child to tell you about the story. Use the story order puzzle to encourage your child to retell the story in the right sequence, in their own words. The correct sequence can be found on the next page.

Help your child think about the messages in the book that go beyond the story and ask: "Would you have given the apple to the donkey or would you have kept it and made a small pie?"

Give your child a chance to respond to the story: "What was your favourite part and why? Were you expecting Tom to have a pie for his mum at the end or was it a surprise?"

Extending learning

Help your child think more about the inferences in the story by asking: "Why do you think Tom is so kind, just like Kitty is?"

In the classroom, your child's teacher may be teaching different kinds of sentences. There are many examples in this book that you could look at with your child, including statements, commands and questions. Find these together and point out how the end punctuation can help us decide what kind of sentence it is.

Franklin Watts
First published in Great Britain in 2020
by The Watts Publishing Group

Series Editors: Jackie Hamley, Melanie Palmer and Grace Glendinning
Series Advisors: Dr Sue Bodman and Glen Franklin
Series Designer: Peter Scoulding and Cathryn Gilbert

A CIP catalogue record for this book is
available from the British Library.

ISBN 978 1 4451 7167 8 (hbk)
ISBN 978 1 4451 7168 5 (pbk)
ISBN 978 1 4451 7296 5 (library ebook)

Printed in China

Franklin Watts
An imprint of
Hachette Children's Group
Part of The Watts Publishing Group
Carmelite House
50 Victoria Embankment
London EC4Y 0DZ

An Hachette UK Company
www.hachette.co.uk

www.reading-champion.co.uk

Answer to Story order: 2, 5, 3, 1, 4